Back-to-School at Home!

Mawuli and Kunale
Book 1

Nadia Edoh

gatekeeper press™
Columbus, OH

Back-to-School at Home!

Published by Gatekeeper Press

2167 Stringtown Rd, Suite 109

Columbus, OH 43123-2989

www.GatekeeperPress.com

Library of Congress Control Number: 2020950377
ISBN (hardcover): 9781662906893
ISBN (paperback): 9781662906909
eISBN: 9781662906916

Thank You

A special and BIG thank you to my sister Amah, also known as Tata to my boys, for believing in me and helping me make this a reality!

Thank you to my boys, Mawuli and Kunale, for the story and for living through it like troopers, and of course to my husband Yusuke for all his support!

The Family

Mawuli and Kunale are brothers, 10 and 5 years old. Their mom was born in Togo and their dad in Japan.

The year 2020 was special for all of them, unlike any other!

Mawuli started fifth grade at home on the computer, and Kunale started kindergarten at home on the computer! Mawuli turned 10 at home, away from his friends, and Kunale turned 5 at home, away from his friends.

They both miss seeing and playing with their friends.

It was a special year indeed!

Mommy kept telling Mawuli and Kunale, "You're living through history. You'll appreciate it one day!"

Puzzles are Mawuli's, Kunale's, and Mommy's favorite thing to do together. Mawuli and Kunale always find the pieces faster than Mommy.

"Here's one!" Mawuli says, holding up a puzzle piece. "We only have four more to go!"

"Here's another one!" Kunale is close behind, plugging another hole in the puzzle.

"Wow, you two are better than me!" Mommy chuckles, while the boys look for the next piece.

Mawuli finds one more puzzle piece, and then Kunale finds the last two, and just like that the puzzle is done.

"We did it!" Mawuli and Kunale say at the same time. They look so happy. Mommy is so proud of them.

"**M**ommy, when can we go back to school?" Mawuli asks Mommy one afternoon. "We've been staying at home for so long … I miss my friends."

Daddy hears Mawuli's question as he walks into the living room.

"Actually, boys, you'll be beginning school in a couple weeks," he explains.

The boys are excited! But there's a twist:

"This year is going to be a little different," Daddy continues. "You will do school at home, on your computers!"

The boys are even more excited. They can already see themselves playing games during school time. They've gotten used to playing on the computer a lot during lockdown!

"Yay!" Mawuli and Kunale say as they jump up and down around Mommy and Daddy.

"I can't wait to see my friends!" Mawuli says.

"I can't wait, either!" Kunale adds.

"This is so exciting," Mommy chimes in. "You might really love it!"

"We are going to school with Daddy to get our computers today. Yay!" says Mawuli.

Mawuli is running down the stairs towards the door.

"Kunale, hurry up! We can't be late!" he shouts back at his little brother as he grabs the face mask Mommy hands him.

"Let's go! Time to pick up your computers!" Daddy is already out the door, heading to the garage.

"I can't wait! I'll get my computer, and I will meet my teacher, too!" says Kunale as he bounces towards the car. He's already wearing his mask. He's so excited!

"They have a schedule for the both of you," Daddy explains. "Mawuli, you are first, and Kunale, you are right after."

And on their way they go, to pick up the computers for back-to-school, at home.

"Thanks, Daddy!" Mawuli says as he takes Daddy's place in front of his new school computer.

"Thanks, Mommy!" Kunale sits across the table from Mawuli, in front of his very own school computer.

"Yay, I'm going to be in kindergarten!" Kunale says.

"Yay, I'm going to start fifth grade!" Mawuli replies.

Kunale is quiet for a minute. And then he looks up at Mommy across the room. "But will I see and play with my friends?"

"You will both see your teachers on the computer and meet your friends on the computer," Mommy tells them. "It's going to be different, but still fun!"

The boys are quiet, they look a bit worried.

"What's the name of your teacher, Kunale?" Mommy asks him, putting her arm around his shoulders.

"Mrs. Dudette," Kunale replies, giggling as he runs away.

"And yours, Mawuli?"

"Mr. Dude!" Mawuli says, smiling from behind the computer.

Mommy smiles and rolls her eyes. "You boys are so silly!"

"Hurry up and eat, boys!" Mommy calls out to Mawuli and Kunale from the living room. "You don't want to be late for your computer meeting with your teacher!"

It's the day everyone has been waiting for: the first day of school. It's finally here!

The boys are sitting at the dining room table. They stuff the last bits of toasted waffle in their mouths, and then they have to clean up quickly, so their friends and teachers won't see a mess in the background when they get on their computers.

"I have to get a small folding table for Kunale so he has his own space," Mommy thinks as she looks at the boys, sitting at either end of the dining room table.

"It's going to be noisy for them to be so close to each other. How will they ever hear their teacher?" Mommy worries.

Kunale's first day is kind of fun, but also ... different.

First, his teacher says hello, and then she explains that everyone is going to introduce themselves.

"Hi, my name is Kunale!" Kunale shouts into the computer, with a big smile on his face.

And then it's his classmates' turn. There's Jason, and Veronica, and Masey. And Sheena, and Hunter, and Anastasia. And ... so many new names, it's hard to remember them all!

After everyone has said their name, the teacher shows them how to read a sight word. And then it's time for a little math. And before you know it, it's break time!

"You have 15 minutes, and then you need to get back in front of the computer!" Mommy explains to Kunale.

That's just enough time for Kunale to eat a snack, go potty, and take out his toys.

While Kunale is playing, a song starts on the computer. It's the teacher, letting Kunale and his friends know that it's time to come back to class!

"Can you jump?" Kunale shouts into the screen. "I can! Watch!" And off he goes, jumping up and down in front of the computer, all the while laughing.

Mawuli is getting annoyed. It's hard to follow what your teacher is saying when your little brother is jumping up and down and laughing and shouting next to you!

"What did you learn today, Mawuli?" Daddy asks when he comes into the kitchen for his lunch break.

"We reviewed some math we did last year," Mawuli explains in between bites of mac and cheese. "The teacher said we will split into breakout groups for a few weeks."

Daddy rubs Kunale's head. "How about you?" he asks.

"I saw Mrs. Dudette, and I got to meet my friends!" Kunale answers.

Mommy calls out from the living room: "Mawuli, can you please come here and show me where we need to go to see the homework?"

After he sits at the computer, Mawuli zips through all the steps, clicking and opening and closing windows super quickly.

"Don't just do it — show us!" Mommy complains to Mawuli as she tries to follow the steps over his shoulder. "Where do we go? On which link do we need to click? If we know, we won't bother you every time!"

Back-to-school at home is tricky for parents, too; they have to learn lots of new things, and make adjustments, also!

One of those adjustments was the small folding table Mommy bought for Kunale, so he and Mawuli wouldn't be too close to each other during class time.

Kunale and Daddy join Mommy and Mawuli around the dining table.

"Did you guys have a good time today?" Daddy asks.

"Yes!" the boys reply at the same time.

It was a good first day of school, even if it was a bit strange.

"**Y**ay!" Mawuli says. "We have PE today — my favorite subject!" He runs out of the living room.

It's the second day of school, and there are even more new things to discover — more new things to get used to.

"I need to have a small ball to bounce around," Mawuli calls out from the other room, as he digs a ball out of a messy pile of toys. "We need a ball for soccer as well."

"How in the world will they play soccer on the computer?" Mommy wonders to herself.

Soon, Mawuli is jumping and bouncing his ball in front of the computer.

Kunale is also at his computer on his little folding table. Mommy is sitting on the floor next to him, looking for the things he needs for school today: dice, some cards, some crayons ….

Kunale watches Mommy dig through the basket of supplies while his teacher speaks on the computer.

"Kunale," Mommy says. She is whispering, so the class won't hear her. "Look at your teacher, not at me!"

"Kunale, listen to the directions she's giving!" Mommy says a moment later.

And again, when she thinks Kunale is speaking too softly, "Kunale, speak up!"

Mommy can't help but give advice to Kunale!

"That was fun!" Mawuli says at the end of the day.

What a funny day back at school!

"We did it!" Mawuli and Kunale each give Mommy a high-five in the living room.

The boys just had their last class of the week.

"Was it a fun week?" Mommy asks. "What did you like the most?"

"You can mute yourself if you don't want to be heard," Mawuli says. "And you can turn off the video if you're not looking all that great and don't want anybody to see you. The teacher doesn't like that, though."

"I love dancing and counting to 100," Kunale says.

"It was easy, and I got to do my homework," Mawuli adds.

"I got to meet my friends," Kunale says.

"Sounds like it was a lot of fun. Great job, you guys!" Mommy says to Mawuli and Kunale.

"It was fun!" Mawuli says. "But I still miss my friends, though."

CPSIA information can be obtained
at www.ICGtesting.com
Printed in the USA
BVHW021538220421
605635BV00007B/1189